POM POM is super

PUFFIN

by Sophy Henn

One morning Pom Pom burst out of bed.
He was **full** of the fidgets
and feeling **fantastic!**

Pom Pom was excited.

So excited . . .

. . . his feet did a little dance
all on their own.

Pom Pom's friends were coming
round to play and he **couldn't wait.**

He got all his best toys ready . . .

and checked the cupboard for snacks.

DING DONG!

went the doorbell.

"They're HERE!"
yelled Pom Pom.

"Hello, Buddy!" said Pom Pom's mummy.

"Wrong!" said Buddy.
"Today I am not just **normal everyday** Buddy, today I am . . .

. . . Buddy the FANTASTIC Footballing FLASH!!!"

And he flashed his fantastic footballing feet all over the place.

"Oooh!" said Pom Pom. "You're a real, proper superhero."

"Yes," said Buddy. "Yes I am."

DING DONG!

went the doorbell . . .

"Greetings! I am
The ANT King!"
boomed Rocco, as he
burst through the door.

"And I'm Swooshing SCOUT
the SPECTACULAR!" said Scout.
"I've got a cape and everything!"

"WOWEEEEEE!"
said Pom Pom. "You are
all ever so SUPER!"

DING DONG!

went the
doorbell . . .

"Well, I just can't imagine who this will be . . ." said Pom Pom's mummy.

"It's me, Twinkly Twirly TORNADO BEAR!" said Baxter, as he twinkled and twirled. "I think it's what I'm BEST at."

And Pom Pom, Buddy, Scout
and Rocco had to agree!

"Come on, everyone! I've got
all the toys ready," said Pom Pom.
"Skipping first . . ."

FLASH
went Buddy.

"Then spaceships . . ."

SWOOSH
went Scout.

"Maybe some marbles . . ."

TWINKLE went Baxter.

". . . and dressing up for afters."

Scurry went Rocco.

"Oh, OK," said Pom Pom. "Maybe you'd like a snack instead?"

"Yes, please!"
said everyone.

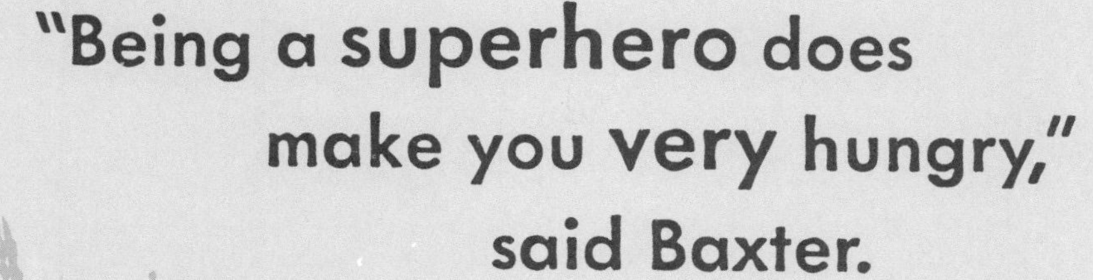

"Being a superhero does make you very hungry," said Baxter.

"Does it?" asked Pom Pom. "I think I'd like to be a superhero, but I'm not sure if I'm super at anything."

"Maybe I'm a
super, BRILLIANT
biscuit juggler!"
said Pom Pom.

"Oops."

"Or maybe I'm a
super-duper
tidy-upper!"

"Hmmm, I'm not sure
I want to be super
at THAT!"

"Oh, I know . . ."

"Lots of **superheroes** can fly,"
said Pom Pom. "What if I **can** too?
That **really** would be **super**!

HERE I GO . . .

1 2

. . . WHEEEEEE!”

"Oh dear," said Pom Pom.
"Maybe I'm just NOT super at all."

"Hang on a tick," said Scout.
"You are **really** good at making
very **LOUD** noises."

"And you are quite **outstanding** at hula-hooping," said Rocco.

"Hey, don't forget you are a **terrific** dancer," said Buddy.

"He's right!" said Baxter.
"You've got some **fantastic** moves!"

"Really?" asked Pom Pom.

"So that means I'm **actually** . . .

"SHOUTY . . .

HULA . . .

DISCO Pom Pom!"

And everyone agreed
that really was
SUP

ER!

For Will, Millie and Felix,
who are all extremely super!
x x x

PUFFIN BOOKS
UK | USA | Canada | Ireland | Australia | India | New Zealand | South Africa
Puffin Books is part of the Penguin Random House group of companies
whose addresses can be found at global.penguinrandomhouse.com.
puffinbooks.com
First published 2016
001

A CIP catalogue record for this book is available from the British Library
Printed in China
Hardback ISBN: 978-0-141-36502-2
Paperback ISBN: 978-0-141-36503-9